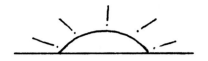

To someone special, a special dedication.
To my one and only sweet darling sister Dianna Henson
who always provided me with nothing but smiles, hugs, and
kisses from the heart. Thanks, I always needed them!

To order additional copies of this book, contact:
Xlibris
1-888-795-4274
www.Xlibris.com
Orders@Xlibris.com

Discover the inspirational magic created from
smiles through the guidance of Mr. Sunny Sunshine.

Nothing but smiles. A comic book.
Written and Illustrated
by
Dwayne S. Henson

1

4

Yes! I struck it rich with lots of happy, happy, smiles. Today really must be my lucky day.
Smile
Smile
Smile

No matter how big or small, you can always send a friend or a loved one a smile through the mail.

Smiles, sometimes they're very hard to control.

Here goes! This time I'm really going to do it. All I need for you to do is to start the countdown from a billion.
Smile

On a bright sunny day, once in a while it's good to just get out and mingle among a friendly colorful crowd of smiles.

24

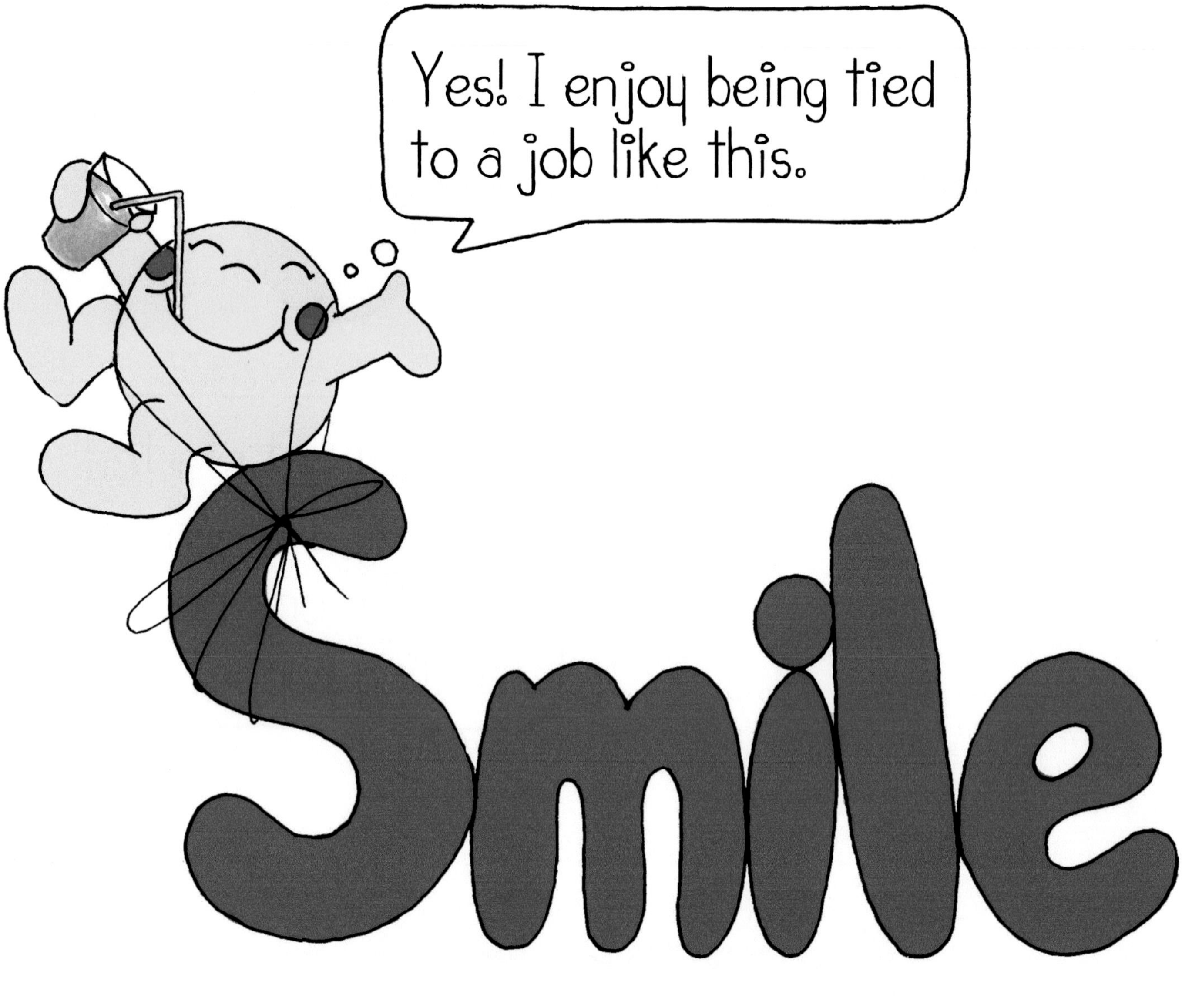
Yes! I enjoy being tied to a job like this.
Smile

I always wanted to see how fast I could go smiling...
Smile
Smile

32

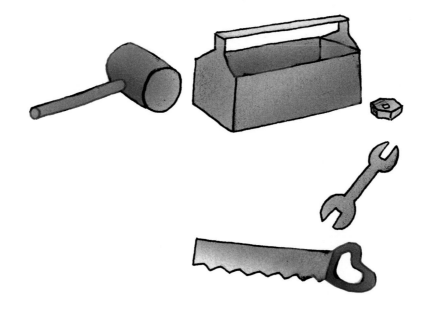

A special offer from
the author / illustrator of the
Mr. Sunny Sunshine books
Dwayne S. Henson

Here's my special offer.
Two preschool educational
books combined in one at
one regular sales price.

For more information on this special offer
and other Mr. Sunny Sunshine books
Contact Xlibris at: 1-888-795-4274

Dwayne S. Henson
Creator of Mr. Sunny Sunshine™

My gift that I would like to share with others is to inspire those who are in need of a smile and to educate others of the positive inspirational value that smiles provide in our society.

With Mr. Sunny Sunshine™ as my tool in this never ending educational smile-based journey, I aim to demonstrate how smiles can be utilized in so many positive encouraging ways such as to inspire, motivate, educate as well as to entertain. How Mr. Sunny Sunshine™ creates smiles and shares them with others, I truly believe, are some of the fascinating trademark dynamics of this inspiring smile making concept.

As you may come to discover there's more inspirational magic behind a smile than what we generally see.

From this unique unit of books you'll learn how and why Mr. Sunny Sunshine™ took it upon himself to create more smiles and inspiration all over the world. Along with this you'll also be provided with a one-of-a-kind, entertaining, smile-based education and much, much, more.

There's a lot to uncover and learn about a smile. I invite you to journey along to see how truly motivating a smile can be.

I certainly hope you enjoy my Mr. Sunny Sunshine™ books as much as I did creating them for others to share. I look forward to creating lots more smiles for many of years to come.

Sincerely, Dwayne S. Henson... Prince of happiness, King of smiles.

Printed in the United States
By Bookmasters